3 4028 09284 2492
HARRIS COUNTY PUBLIC LIBRARY

D1378464

First American edition published in 2005 by Lerner Publishing Group, Inc.

Originally published in 2004 by Orchard Books, London, England

Carolrhoda Books
A division of Lerner Publishing Group, Inc.
241 First Avenue North
Minneapolis, MN 55401 USA

For reading levels and more information,
look up this title at www.lernerbooks.com

For Natalie, Madeleine, and Eòin —M.M.

For Jay and Danny —A.A.

Library of Congress Cataloging-in-Publication Data

Mayo, Margaret, 1935–
Choo choo clickety-clack! / by Margaret Mayo ; illustrated by Alex Ayliffe.— 1st American ed.
p. cm.
Originally published in 2004 by Orchard Books, London, England.
Summary: Rhythmic sounds imitate trains, planes, and other busy transports that come and go.
ISBN: 978-1-57505-819-1 (lib. bdg. : alk. paper)
[1. Transportation—Fiction. 2. Noise—Fiction.] I. Ayliffe, Alex, ill. II. Title.
PZ7.M47366Ch 2005
[E]—dc22 2004011976

Printed and bound in China
6–OS–12/1/14

CHOO CHOO Clickety-Clack!

written by Margaret Mayo • illustrated by Alex Ayliffe

Carolrhoda Books / Minneapolis

102

Trains are great at speed, speed, **speeding,**

Through tunnels rumbling, over tracks rattling,

All aboard, at stations stopping.

Choo choo, clickety-clack! Off they go!

Airplanes are great at fly, fly, **flying,**
To faraway places, people carrying,
Down runways—up, up, and away—soaring.
RoarrrRR! Off they go!

Cars are great at drive, drive, **driving,**
To stores or friends or special outings,
Trunk packing, seat calling, belts fastening.
Beep, beep! Off they go!

Race cars are great at race, race, **racing,**
Waiting at the starting line, crouching, growling,
Hurtling around the track, chase, chase, chasing.
Zoom, zoom! Off they go!

36
36

86

Sailboats are great at sail, sail, **sailing,**
Over waves bouncing, splishing, splashing,
Water slapping, sails flapping.
Flappety-flap! Off they go!

Hot-air balloons are great at float, float, **floating**,

High in the sky, riding, gliding,

Heating, filling, swelling, rising.

Whoooosh! Off they go!

Motorbikes are great at rev, rev, **revving,**
Turning, swerving, speeding, passing,
Slowing down — no crashing!
Vroom, vroom! Off they go!

S
5
D2
5

Bikes are great at whiz, whiz, **whizzing,**

Needing no engines, just pedals for pushing,

Feet pumping, wheels whirling.

Zippety-zip! Off they go!

Cable cars are great at climb, climb, climbing,

Up the mountain swiftly, swinging.

Hurry in, skiers—doors closing.

Shlummp! Whurrrr! Off they go!

Buses are great at go, go, **going**,
Same route driving, same time arriving,
Waiting, flagging, stopping, starting.
Ding, ding! Off they go!

61

Ferryboats are great at load, load, **loading,**

Cars parking, people boarding,

Ready to go! Toot, toot, whistle sounding.

Chug, chug! Off they go!

Now it is dark— many vehicles are resting.
But through the night, some keep on traveling,
Still *zippety-zipping* and clickety-clacking.
On they go, till they are **home at last!**